An Unlikely Ballerina

For Anna, whose dancing has enriched my life.
—K.P.G.

To Akine Hosoda, Yu Ito, Saki Mizutani, Mizuki Nishiyama, Hiyori Sakakibara,
Miyabi Sato, Rina Suita, and Runa Yamashita for their devoted support and creativity.
—C.K.

ACKNOWLEDGMENTS
I first learned the inspiring story of Lily Marks at the breathtaking exhibit "Diaghiliev
and the Ballets Russes, 1909-1929: When Art Danced with Music" at Washington, D.C.'s
National Gallery in September 2013. That same season Tina Sutton's biography *The
Making of Markova* was published. I'm very grateful to have had Sutton's book, along
with the 1953 memoir, *Alicia Markova: Her Life and Art*, by Markova's longtime dance
partner, Anton Dolin (originally Pat Kay), as my sources for the writing of this book.
—K.P.G.

The images in this book are used with the permission of: © Hulton-Deutsch Collection/
CORBIS/Getty Images, p. 32 (top); Bettmann/Getty Images, p. 32 (bottom).

KAR-BEN PUBLISHING, INC.
A division of Lerner Publishing Group, Inc.
241 First Avenue North
Minneapolis, MN 55401 USA
1-800-4-KARBEN
Website address: www.karben.com

Main body text is set in Breughel Com 55 Roman 15/20.
Typeface provided by Linotype AG.

Library of Congress Cataloging-in-Publication Data

Names: Goddu, Krystyna Poray, author. | Kawa, Cosei, illustrator.
Title: The unlikely ballerina / by Krystyna Poray Goddu ; illustrated by Cosei Kawa.
Description: Minneapolis : Kar-Ben Publishing, [2018] | Series: Jewish heroes |
    Summary: "A small, frail girl with wobbly legs and turned-out toes became the first
    Jewish prima ballerina assoluta in history, Alicia Markova"— Provided by publisher.
    Includes facts about Markova's life.
Identifiers: LCCN 2017030090| ISBN 9781512483628 (lb) | ISBN 9781512483635 (pb) |
    ISBN 9781541524071 (eb pdf)
Subjects: LCSH: Markova, Alicia, Dame, 1910-2004—Juvenile fiction. | CYAC:
    Markova, Alicia, Dame, 1910-2004—Fiction. | Ballet dancers—Fiction. |
    Jews—Fiction.
Classification: LCC PZ7.1.G616 b Unl 2018 | DDC [E]—dc23

LC record available at https://lccn.loc.gov/2017030090

Manufactured in the United States of America
1-43361-33173-10/25/2017

An Unlikely Ballerina

Krystyna Poray Goddu

ILLUSTRATIONS BY
Cosei Kawa

KAR-BEN
PUBLISHING

Little Lily Marks
loved to stand on her tiptoes.

She would stand still for what
seemed like forever, then tiptoe
lightly around the room.

But as Lily grew older, her parents noticed that she walked awkwardly, with her feet pointing out.

The doctor gave her clunky lace-up shoes to wear. Lily almost cried when she saw them. She wanted pretty slippers, like her sisters had. And the shoes didn't even help! Her feet still seemed to go in different directions, and sometimes her right leg buckled under her.

The doctor recommended iron braces to strengthen and straighten Lily's legs. The leg braces looked even more ugly and uncomfortable than the shoes! "Isn't there anything we can do instead?" her mother pleaded.

The doctor thought for a moment. "Would you be willing to try an experiment?" he asked.

Lily and her mother both nodded eagerly.

"You could try dancing lessons."

Lily and her mother were both astonished. But Lily would do anything to avoid the braces.

To her surprise, Lily loved her dance classes. She did exercises at the barre and learned many dance steps. Her legs grew stronger. "Dancing lessons are the nicest kind of medicine!" Lily told her mother.

Her teacher noticed how quickly Lily mastered even the most complicated steps. "She has natural talent," the teacher told Lily's mother. "She never even seems to get out of breath! She should have private lessons."

"I'm glad to see her legs getting stronger," Lily's mother replied. "But I don't expect her to become a real dancer."

At home, Lily taught her three little sisters to
dance. They put on elaborate performances.
Their great-grandfather, who made and sold theater
costumes, taught Lily how to make fancy costumes for
herself and her sisters. Lily knew she was his favorite because
her middle name, Alicia, had been her great-grandmother's.

Lily's father built a stage in the backyard. Neighbors came to watch the sisters perform their shows. "Look how beautifully Lily dances!" they whispered.

One day Lily's teacher said, "Lily is ready to dance on a real stage." She wanted the girl to enter a local talent competition. But her parents were worried. Could their fragile eight-year-old daughter perform in front of strangers?

At the competition,
Lily danced gracefully
to a sad waltz. The
audience wept—then
applauded wildly. She
won first prize.

The audience's reaction made Lily very proud. Her
surprised parents realized their talented daughter should
have private lessons after all. Now Lily worked harder
than ever at her dancing.

She let nothing stop her from doing her very best
on stage. Nobody knew she was suffering from
chicken pox when she starred in the dancing
school's performance of *The Arabian Nights*.
Newspaper critics noticed only her talent.

When Lily was
nine years old,
her mother told
her a secret.

"When I was expecting you, I saw
the famous Russian ballerina Anna
Pavlova dance. She was magnificent!
And I made a secret wish that I'd
have a baby girl who would one day
dance as beautifully as Pavlova."

"And look," she continued excitedly. "The great Pavlova is going to perform here in London! Now you'll have the chance to see her dance!"

Lily's father offered to take her to the show.

A few nights later, Lily watched, hypnotized, as Pavlova performed. The ballerina was tiny and dark-haired, just like Lily. And—although nobody knew it—Pavlova, like Lily, was Jewish.

As she twirled, the red and yellow silk petals of her costume transformed her into a blooming flower. Then, with the music fading, Pavlova drew the petals over her face one by one until the flower closed in on itself.

Lily turned to her father. "I have to meet her! Papa, please arrange it—please!"

At intermission, Lily's father ran backstage. "May I bring my daughter to Pavlova's dressing room after the performance?" he asked the ballerina's manager.

"Ah, no," the manager replied, "Madame never receives guests in her dressing room."

But Lily's father wouldn't give up. "My daughter is a talented dancer. Meeting Pavlova is her greatest wish."

A young dancer? The manager smiled. "Bring her to Ivy House tomorrow. She can dance for Madame."

While her father pleaded, Lily waited anxiously in her seat, devouring the photos of Pavlova in the program. At last, her father returned with the astonishing news that she would dance for Pavlova the next day.

Then she and her father joined the adoring crowd at the stage door, waiting to see Pavlova emerge. Elegantly dressed gentlemen carried bouquet after bouquet of flowers to the ballerina's waiting limousine.

Finally, Pavlova appeared,
her face nearly hidden by an
enormous hat. She climbed
into the limousine and, as it
pulled away, tossed roses and
carnations out the window
to her admirers.

The next morning Lily and her father took the train into the countryside. Lily clutched the bag her mother had packed with her best practice clothes. Would she be able to dance her very best for Pavlova?

Lily and her father walked up to the grand house—past a pond with a bubbling fountain and graceful swans, past gardens of colorful flowers and stately trees. Pavlova met them at the door and welcomed them warmly.

In the dance studio, Pavlova instructed Lily through a series of exercises. Lily's once-weak legs moved with strength and grace.

When she finished, the famous ballerina smiled.
"You could become a fine dancer," she said.

Lily's heart beat faster.

"But," added Pavlova, "your life will be hard work,
and you must be prepared to give up many pleasures."

At that moment, Lily
promised herself that
she would devote her life
to the ballet she loved.

Lily Marks never forgot Pavlova's words. In time, the little girl who had once struggled to walk became Alicia Markova, one of the greatest ballerinas in the world.

Afterword

Lillian Alicia Marks was born in London, England in 1910. She was the first of four daughters born to Arthur Marks, a Jewish engineer, and Eileen Barry, an Irish Catholic who converted to Judaism.

From the moment she decided to become a ballerina, Lily devoted her life to ballet. She made her professional debut at age ten. When she was 14, she was selected to join the Ballets Russes, a famous dance company. The company's famous director, Serge Diaghilev, changed her name to the more Russian-sounding Alicia Markova because the world's most well-known ballerinas at the time were Russian. He thought no one would want to see a British ballerina dance. Lily became the youngest-ever soloist at the Ballets Russes.

Later, Lily danced internationally. In the 1940s she was the prima ballerina for the US dance company that became the American Ballet Theatre. She founded several dance companies, served as ballet director for the Metropolitan Opera House in New York, and taught around the world. She performed in Israel with Festival Ballet and danced at benefit concerts to raise money for the Mann Auditorium in Tel Aviv.

Lily gave up much for her art, as she had promised herself that day at Anna Pavlova's Ivy House. She never married. For many years she traveled the world dancing, with no permanent home. Admirers noted many similarities between Lily and the ballerina who had inspired her. Both were small and dark-haired. Both were Jewish (although Pavlova never publicly revealed her heritage and Lily was outspoken in her love for Judaism). Both seemed to dance effortlessly, with extraordinary lightness and technical skill.

The small, frail girl with wobbly legs and turned-out toes became the first Jewish *prima ballerina assoluta* in history, inspiring countless young dancers both before and after her death in 2004.

(Top) Alicia Markova at age 13 in 1923.
(Bottom) Alicia Markova, in character and en pointe.